To Daniel, who has sat with me in the dark and led me back to the light more times than I can recount.

The Moonsweep

WRITTEN AND ILLUSTRATED
BY
SARAH A. COOLS

It has long been rumored that the moon is covered in a layer of dust. Whoever started this rumor somehow forgot to mention that there is also a Moonsweep.

moonsweep is much like her cousins on earth, the himneysweeps, but instead of cleaning out chimneys and luepipes, the little sweep on ne moon dusts out the craters nd sweeps the craggy surface of the spinning orb. It's an endless job that must be attended to day after day.

One day as she
swept around the
deepest of the
craters, the
Moonsweep tripped
and tumbled
backwards …

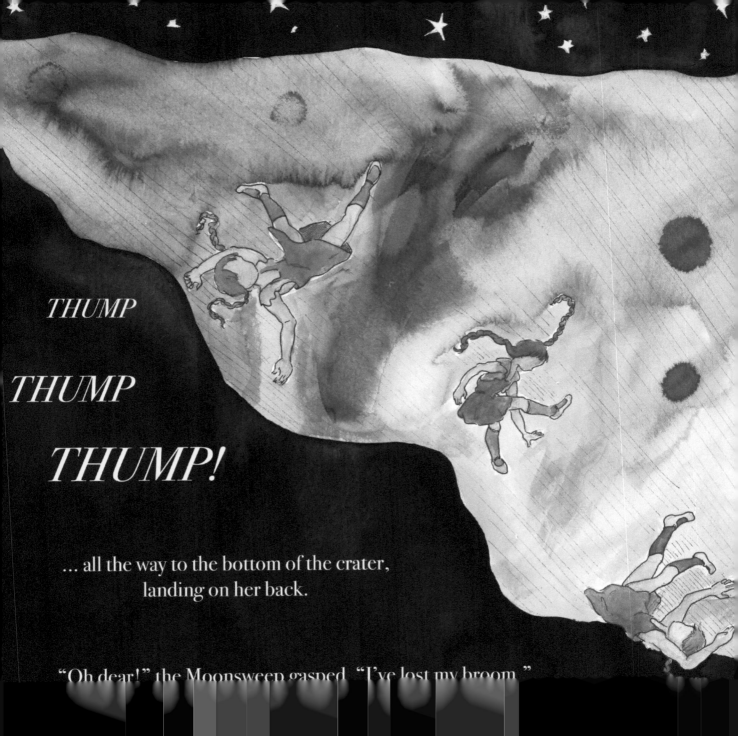

THUMP

THUMP

THUMP!

... all the way to the bottom of the crater,
landing on her back.

"Oh dear!" the Moonsweep gasped. "I've lost my broom."

It was too dark down in the pit to see, so the Moonsweep
crawled on her hands and knees, searching for her broom.
As she patted the ground in search of her broom, puffs of
dust billowed up and stung her eyes.

"Where did all this dust come from?" she cried
out. "I've swept out this crater so many times, there can't
possibly be this much dust left! Will it never go away?"

She sat in the dust and darkness and began to cry.

After what seemed like a long time, the Moonsweep felt something warm and wet touch her hand. She jumped up. A moon-fox sat at her feet, its pale fur glowing gently and its nose reaching to nudge her hand again.

"What-what are you doing here?" she stammered, rubbing her teary eyes.

"I heard you crying and came to join you," the Fox said.

"Can you get me out of here?" sniffled the Moonsweep.

"Out of where?" the pale Fox asked, head cocked. "Out of crying?"

The Moonsweep laughed, but saw the Fox was serious. "No," she said, "out o
this hole. I don't think you can fix what's making me cry. I can't even fix it myself and
that's the whole problem."

She began to cry again
remembering her lost broom
and her tumble into the hole
and the hopelessly impossible
task of cleaning it out.

The Fox and the Moonsweep sat in the dark awhile, the girl crying into her hands and the Fox with its head in her lap.

Way up above the tiniest sliver of the Sun peeked over the crater's dark rim. The Moonsweep felt a drip on her foot and looked up to see a tear rolling down the Fox's cheek.

She started. "Why are you crying?" she asked in surprise.

"I can feel how your heart aches, and I know it is because you feel your work is not enough. Isn't that right?" the Fox asked gently.

"H-h-how did you know?" the Moonsweep stuttered, wiping her own tears away and staring in confusion at the glowing fox.

"I've seen how hard you work every day to keep the moon clean and glowing; I admired your dedication. When I saw you tumble down here, I thought perhaps you were hurt at first," the Fox said.

The Moonsweep sniffed and nodded, rubbing her red eyes to try to stem the tears. "But why does that make you cry?" she asked.

"But now I see that your pain is from within. You are sad because you think our work will never be finished and you've failed."

The Fox licked her face. "Because you can't see how beautiful your work is. No matter how much or how little it looks, it is still wonderful, because you keep at it."

A twinkling warmth budded in the Moonsweep's chest. She felt its light war her from the inside out, drying her tears before they fell. "You really think so?" sh sniffed.

The Fox grinned. "I know so!"

"Shall we leave this hole now?" the Fox asked.
"I can't leave without my broom," the girl
hesitated.
Nose to the ground, the Fox ran a little way
away into the dark, sniffing, and returned in a
moment with the wooden broom in its mouth.
Elated, the Moonsweep hugged the Fox.

Hand in paw, they climbed up the crater and out the other side, back into the light.

As the Moonsweep returned to her dusting, the Fox trailed behind her chasing shooting stars.

All was well for a while for the Moonsweep had the words and company of her friend to keep her spirit strong. However, the longer she worked, the more absorbed she became with her broom and the dust.

She didn't notice that her work was taking her to the dark side of the moon, where the light disappeared and the dust grew cold.

Before she realized it,
she was in the deepest,
darkest part.

"Why isn't my moon glowing?" she said
in shock to the Fox. "I've been dusting so
steadily just as you told me to - not too
fast and not too slow, but just steady. So
why is my moon all dark?"

"You don't know?" The Fox looked amused. "Well, come with me." And he bounded away.

As the Moonsweep chased after him, up ahead where she hadn't yet swept, something caught her eye. A shimmering light flickered on the horizon. "What is that?" she gasped. "What could be making my moon glow?"

"Come and see!" the Fox grinned. The Moonsweep took off running toward the light. It grew brighter and she saw that the ground ahead was glowing more brightly than she'd ever seen it.

All at once, she was in the middle of the glow which she found was radiating from high above her in the blanket of space. The Sun hung overhead, its light cascading down, washing the moon, the girl and the Fox in its majestic light.

The Moonsweep's
mouth fell open.

"Oh, how beautiful you are!" she whispered in awe.

The Sun smiled down at her. "I have been waiting for
you," it said.

"For me?" the Moonsweep asked in astonishment.

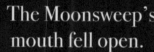

The Moonsweep looked back behind her and could make out the shadows from which she had come. Looking ahead to where the ground glowed under her feet, she was surprised to find there was dust here, but her moon still shone.

"Please, can you tell me something?" she asked the Sun.

The Sun smiled in assent.

"How is it that my moon is glowing, but I haven't dusted it?"

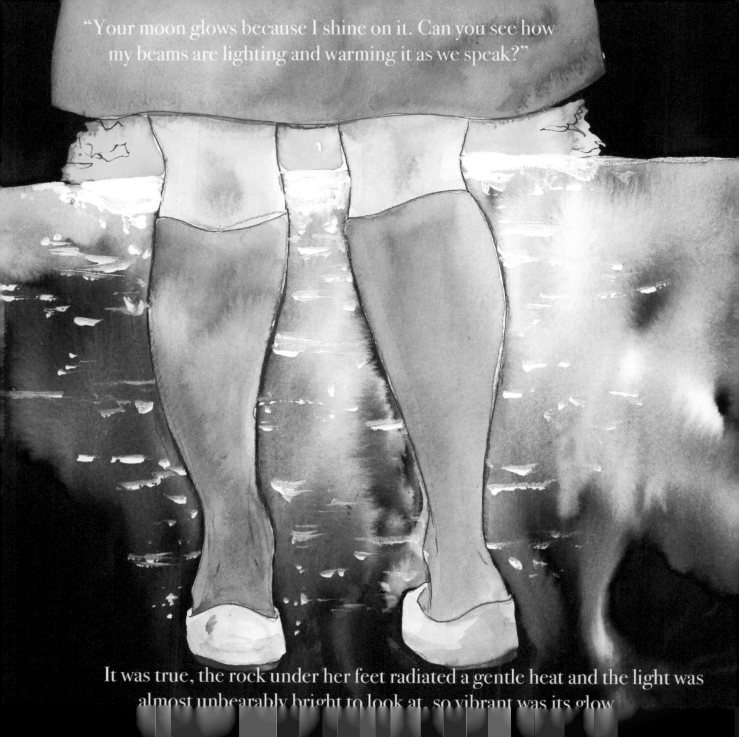

"Your moon glows because I shine on it. Can you see how my beams are lighting and warming it as we speak?"

It was true, the rock under her feet radiated a gentle heat and the light was almost unbearably bright to look at, so vibrant was its glow.

"But the Fox told me what I did was important." The Moonsweep looked at the Fox reproachfully, her bottom lip quivering again.

"It is important!" the Fox barked, looking from the girl to the Sun.

"But if the Sun is the one who makes my moon glow, why do I work at all? My dusting is useless!"

A beam of light reached out and touched her cheek in a reassuring manner. The Sun smiled again and spoke softly.

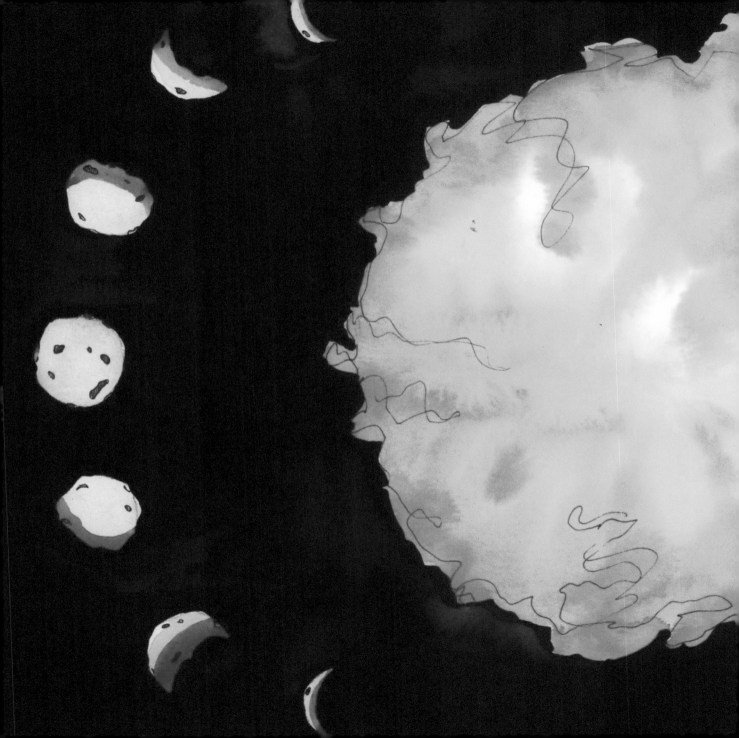

"My light makes your moon, and all others,
shine in the darkness.
I am the reason for the warmth on your skin.
I keep the galaxies from freezing.
I make the dust sparkle as it falls into space."

"If you do all that," the Moonsweep said, "why do I need to sweep the dust off the moon?"

"When you sweep," the Sun answered, "it causes my light to be reflected to the stars. It is important that you work on your moon."

"I help the stars to see your light?" the Moonsweep gasped, suddenly growing excited.

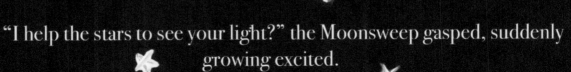

"Indeed," the Sun said, very pleased.

"How will I know if it reaches the stars?"

"It reaches everywhere that I
desire my light to fall," the
Sun's voice rumbled.

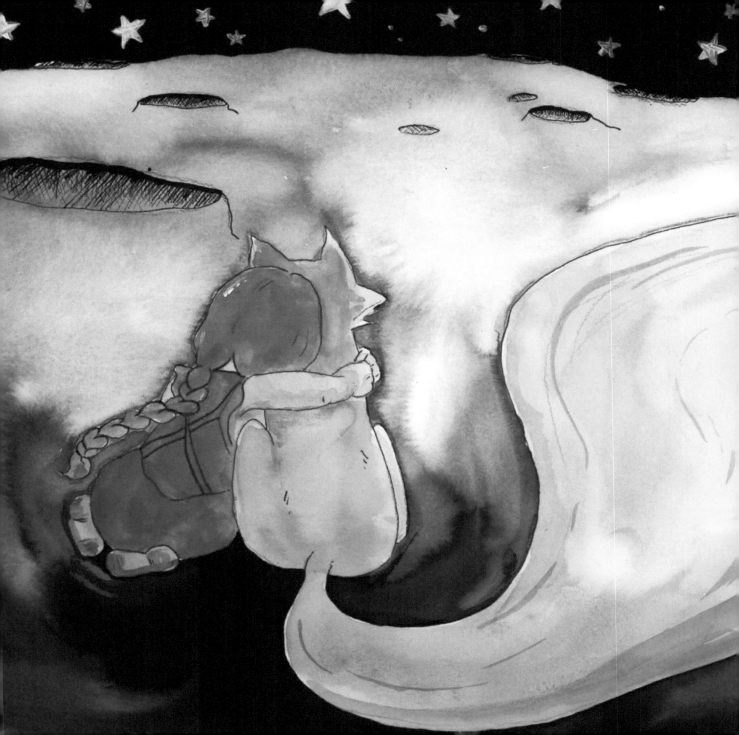

Lowering her broom, the Moonsweep gazed at the Sun, its light too marvelous to look at without making her eyes water.

She blinked, smiling once again.

"I will keep dusting; I think I now know why it is important." She hugged the Fox and he grinned from her to the Sun, his pale tail swishing in glee.

"You'll always keep shining though, won't you?" the Moonsweep questioned. "Even if I don't keep up with my dusting?"

"I *have* always shone,

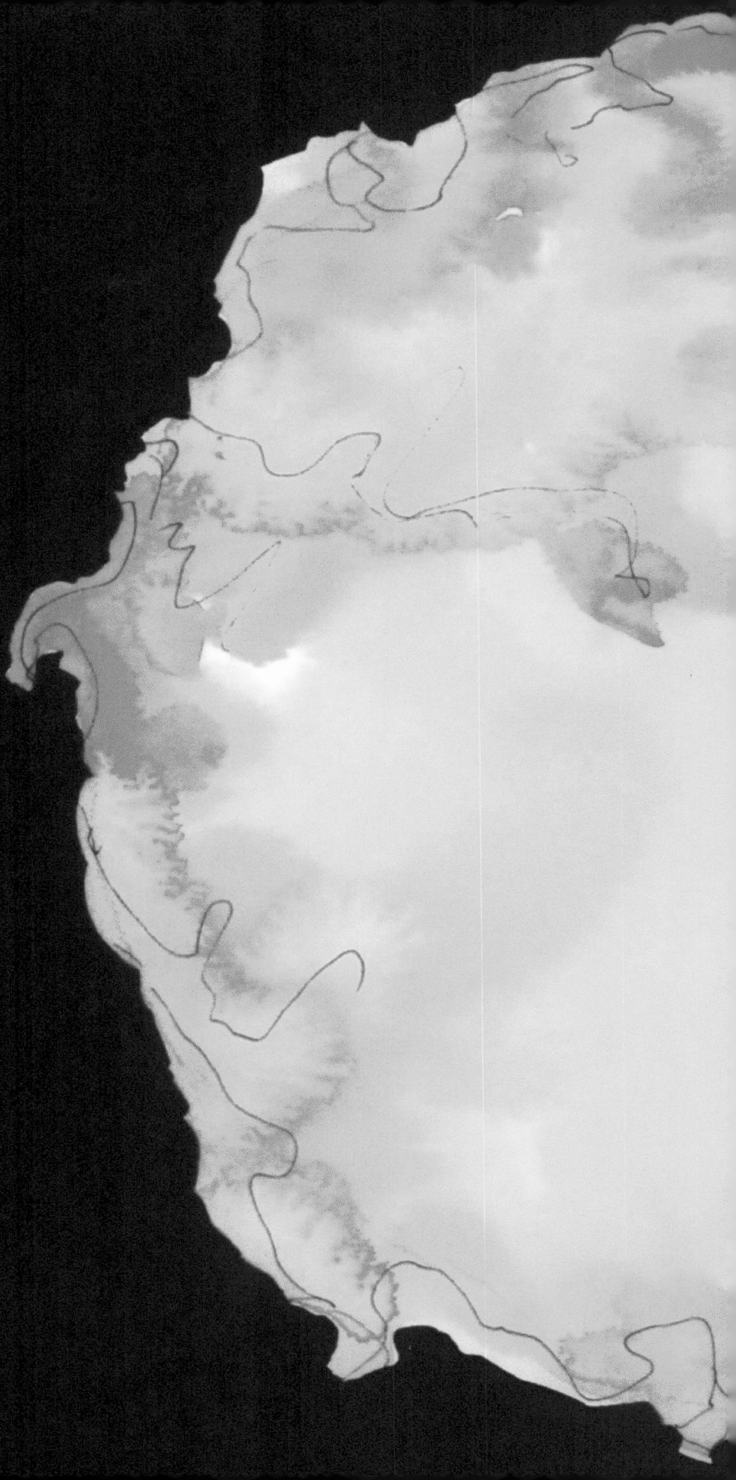

I *am* always shining,

And I *will* always shine,"
the Sun said.

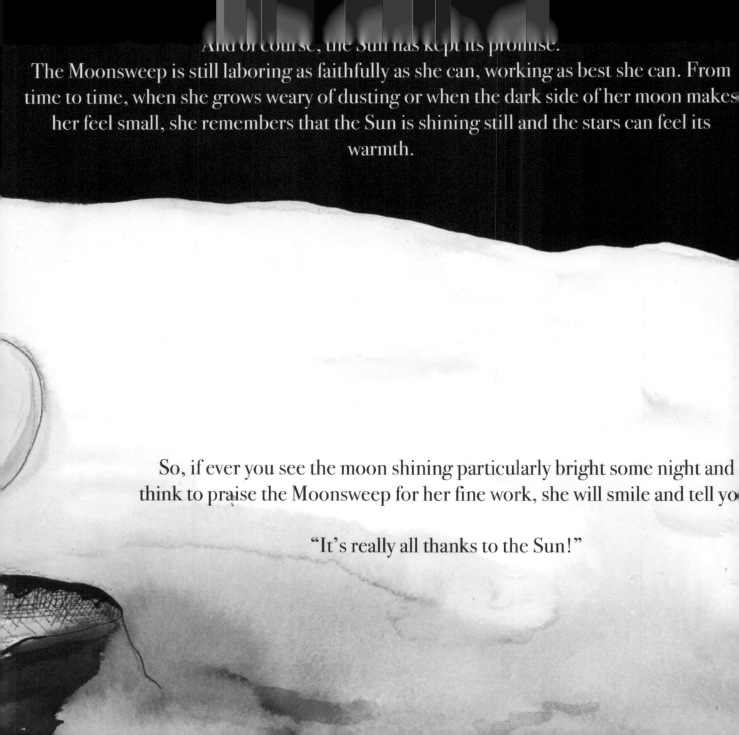

And of course, the Sun has kept its promise.
The Moonsweep is still laboring as faithfully as she can, working as best she can. From time to time, when she grows weary of dusting or when the dark side of her moon makes her feel small, she remembers that the Sun is shining still and the stars can feel its warmth.

So, if ever you see the moon shining particularly bright some night and think to praise the Moonsweep for her fine work, she will smile and tell you

"It's really all thanks to the Sun!"

THE END

CPSIA information can be obtained
at www.ICGtesting.com
Printed in the USA
LVHW070922220221
679611LV00031B/995